Bad Rat!

Level 1A

Written by Karen Wallace
Illustrated by Rachael O'Neill
Reading Consultant: Betty Franchi

About Phonics

Spoken English uses more than 40 speech sounds. Each sound is called a *phoneme*. Some phonemes relate to a single letter (d-o-g) and others to combinations of letters (sh-ar-p). When a phoneme is written down, it is called a *grapheme*. Teaching these sounds, matching them to their written form, and sounding out words for reading is the basis of phonics.

Early phonics instruction gives children the tools to sound out, blend, and say the words without having to rely on memory or guesswork. This instruction gives children the confidence and ability to read unfamiliar words, helping them progress toward independent reading.

About the Consultant

Betty Franchi is an American educator with
a Bachelor's Degree in Elementary and Middle
Education as well as a Master's Degree in Special
Education. Betty holds a National Boards for
Professional Teaching Standards certification.
Throughout her 24 years as a teacher, she has
studied and developed an expertise in Phonetic
Awareness and has implemented phonetic strategies,
teaching many young children to read, including
students with special needs.

Reading tips

 This book focuses on the sounds:
s, a, t, p, i, n, c, e, h, r, m, d, g, o, u, l, f, and *b.*

Tricky and/or new words in this book

Any words in bold may have unusual spellings
or are new and have not yet been introduced.

> **Tricky and/or new words in this book**
>
> **I   me   my   see
> said   the   to   you**

Extra ways to have fun with this book

After the readers have finished the story, ask them
questions about what they have just read.

Where did Rat hide the bun?
How many different places did Rat hide?

Make flashcards of the focus sounds (s, a, t, p, i, n, c, e,
h, r, m, d, g, o, u, l, f, and b). Ask the reader to say the
sounds. This will help reinforce letter/sound matches.

Reading is fun!
I love to read with my
mom, snuggled up in bed.
She always says "Good job!"
when I read.

A Pronunciation Guide

This grid highlights the sounds used in the story and offers a guide on how to say them.

s	a	t	p
as in sat	as in ant	as in tin	as in pig
i	n	c	e
as ink	as in net	as in cat	as in egg
h	r	m	d
as in hen	as in rat	as in mug	as in dog
g	o	u	l
as in get	as in ox	as in up	as in log
f	b	j	v
as in fan	as in bag	as in jug	as in van
w	z	y	k
as in wet	as in zip	as in yet	as in kit
qu	x	ff	ll
as in quiz	as in box	as in off	as in fill
ss	zz	ck	
as in hiss	as in buzz	as in duck	

Be careful not to add an /uh/ sound to /s/, /t/, /p/, /c/, /h/, /r/, /m/, /d/, /g/, /l/, /f/ and /b/. For example, say /ff/ not /fuh/ and /sss/ not /suh/.

Rat hid a bun in his bed.

"**My** bun!" **said** Pig **to** Fat Cat.

"**The** bad rat has my bun!"

"Let **me** get Rat!" said Fat Cat.

Fat Cat ran to the red hut.

Rat hid in a pot!

Rat hid in a hat!

Rat hid in a cup!

Fat Cat sat on the rug.

"**I** can **see you**, Rat," said Fat Cat.
Tug! Tug!

"Give me the bun, Rat.
Pig is mad," said Fat Cat.

"The bun is in the bed," said Rat.

Pig has his bun.

Bad Rat!

OVER **48** TITLES IN SIX LEVELS
Betty Franchi recommends...

Other titles to enjoy from Level 1

I love reading phonics — Clint and Grant **Play I-Spy**

I love reading phonics — **The Best Gift**

I love reading phonics — **Bret and Grandma's Trip!**

978 1 84898 752 4   978 1 84898 750 0   978 1 84898 751 7

Some titles from Level 2

I love reading phonics — **Wish Fish**

I love reading phonics — **Chuck and Duck**

I love reading phonics — **Pink Bunny**

I love reading phonics — **Let's go to the Swings**

978 1 84898 755 5   978 1 84898 756 2   978 1 84898 760 9   978 1 84898 759 3

Some titles from Level 3

I love reading phonics — **Bart's Go-Cart**

I love reading phonics — **Queen Ella's Feet**

I love reading phonics — **Puff Flies**

I love reading phonics — **The Pop Duet**

978 1 84898 768 5   978 1 84898 764 7   978 1 84898 765 4   978 1 84898 767 8

An Hachette Company
First Published in the United States by TickTock, an imprint of Octopus Publishing Group.
www.octopusbooksusa.com

Copyright © Octopus Publishing Group Ltd 2013

Distributed in the US by
Hachette Book Group USA
237 Park Avenue, New York NY 10017, USA

Distributed in Canada by
Canadian Manda Group
165 Dufferin Street, Toronto, Ontario, Canada M6K 3H6

ISBN 978 1 84898 747 0

Printed and bound in China
10 9 8 7 6 5 4 3 2 1